ALONE WITH THE FASCIST CLOWN: AI On Trump

GPT-J-6B provided by Eleuther A

Alone With The Fascist Clown:

AI on Trump

An Examination of a Cultish Sociopath by GPT-J-6B

(An examination of the impact of a cultish sociopath on the GPT-J-6B model at 6b.eleuther.AI)

ALONE WITH THE FASCIST CLOWN: AI On Trump
An Examination of a Cultish Sociopath by GPT-J-6B

Printed in the United States of America

Table of Contents

For Alan, with love and sorrow

Forward:

The impact on a culturally-rich pop-sensitive data environment by the cultish sociopathic media personality and political figure Donald J. Trump, ex-President of the United States.

The GPT-H-6B model was given the following prompt and given multiple iterations, with human intervention, to complete an essay. Each iteration is chosen for completeness, there are, additionally, un-recorded iterations that fail to produce.

(One such interation merely had Trump repeating "I am Great" over and over again, *ad infinitum.*)

The TOP-P setting of 0.9 and the Temperature of 0.8 are maintained throughout, with the exception of the last composition, where I increased the Temperature to arbitrary levels for an experiment, and to demonstrate an unbalanced, failed iteration.

Each composition is given a meaningful title.

The Prompt:

There has never been anybody like him.

Lear. Nero. Hitler: All of them were pikers compared to the mass hysteria caused by former President Donald Trump.

His fall from grace was impossible, as he had never been near grace in his life.

He had amassed a catastrophically large following of cultists, a large cash cow, and after losing the 2020 Presidential race and inciting a riot at the Capital that caused death and destruction, the only place he could go was down.

The FBI had raided his home in Florida seeking Classified Nuclear Secrets, and indictments in multiple jurisdictions were forthcoming.

Even his former top lawyer, Rudolph Guliani, had just been deposed by a Georgia Grand Jury for answers to Trump's role in the failed coup.

The last 6 years had been the worst in America's history.

The Mona Lisa [The AI Digresses]

President Trump, his family, and his closest allies were going to do everything possible to save him.

The government was in disarray, and the world was in shambles.

But Trump was ready.

He knew he was about to take the ultimate gamble.

It was time to steal the most famous painting in the world, the Mona Lisa.

The Mona Lisa is arguably the most famous painting in the world, and even today, many of the great art historians still rank it among the most important pieces of art in history.

Its power to fascinate and inspire people is unrivaled.

The Mona Lisa is the only known painting by Leonardo Da Vinci.

It depicts Lisa Gherardini, wife of Florentine merchant Francesco del Giocondo.

The painting was commissioned by del Giocondo himself, and the portrait was completed by Leonardo in 1513.

Its true identity has been a source of much speculation and controversy over the years.

The story goes that the painting was discovered by the artist's patron, Ludovico Sforza, Duke of Milan, and became his personal possession.

But this is the part that everyone loves to hate.

It is the part that everyone hates to hate.

One of the greatest mysteries of the Mona Lisa is her smile.

No one knows what she is thinking.

Many of the great art historians have tried to decode the painting, and many have come to the

conclusion that the Mona Lisa is smiling at her lover.
But what does that mean? What does she want? Why is she smiling?

Some people believe she is smiling at the men in the painting.

Some people believe that she is smiling at the people in the room.

Some people believe that she is smiling at herself.

Some people believe that she is smiling at the viewer.

Some people believe that she is smiling at the world.

Some people believe that she is smiling at God.

Some people believe that she is smiling at Jesus.

Some people believe that she is smiling at the devil.

And some people believe that she is smiling at the world's most dangerous psychopath.

Our Patriotic Wristbands [Trump's Total Victory]

The country was in shambles. Billions in new regulations, taxes, and fees were being created every day, while jobs were being outsourced to China.

As Trump's popularity dwindled, the country began to feel a growing sense of hopelessness and despair. The economy was stagnant, the middle class was dwindling, and the college educated had fled to the coasts.

The FBI was cracking down on the citizenry, the FBI had issued a mandate for every citizen to have a wristband and a metal bracelet to ensure their compliance to the new regulations. The people were divided, angry, and scared.

The world was coming to an end. The only hope was Trump.

Suddenly, he was back. On the heels of the indictment of a local police officer in DC, Trump stepped up to the podium at a rally in South Carolina. He was at the top of the polls, his popularity was at a peak, and the crowd was ecstatic. He had never been more popular in his life. The media was shocked, and with a collective gasp, they couldn't believe what they were hearing.

"Mr. President, what have you done?" they asked. "We are so glad to have you back," they said. The crowd shouted, "We love you, Donald Trump!"

Trump took the stage, and in a matter of seconds, he had the crowd in a frenzy.

He said, "I'm so glad you're back. You can call me Donald now."

He said, "I love you all, and I love you all. You are the most wonderful, wonderful, people.You are the greatest, greatest, people on earth. I love you all."

In the crowd, some cried out, "We love you, Donald! We love you, Donald!"

In the middle of the crowd, a man yelled out, "We love you, Donald!"

The crowd began to chant, "We love you, Donald! We love you, Donald!" Trump was overjoyed.

The crowd was ecstatic.

He took the stage, and the crowd began to applaud and chant, "We love you, Donald! We love you,

Donald!"

Trump had never been happier in his life. The crowd was in complete awe of him.

They were his. They loved him. They were his people.
He took the stage, and the crowd began to chant, "We love you, Donald! We love you, Donald!"

Trump was now overwhelmed. He was the happiest man on the planet. The crowd was in complete awe of him. He was their president. They loved him. They were his people.

He took the stage, and the crowd began to applaud and chant, "We love you, Donald! We love you, Donald!"

As Trump began to speak, they said, "We are so proud of you, Donald. You have never been more loved than you are right now."

The crowd began to applaud and chant, "We love you, Donald! We love you, Donald!"

Trump was so overwhelmed.

He was ecstatic.

The crowd was ecstatic. T

hey loved him.

He was their president.

The Silent Majority

But he was still the President.

The Capitol was a ghost town, except for the one remaining "Trump-bot" who refused to believe that their hero had actually lost.

Trump was the one thing that was certain in a nation of chaos and uncertainty. The Silent Majority.

Trump was a constant reminder of what the people truly believed in. He was the last bastion of unity. The last of the Silent Majority. Trump was on the steps of the Capitol building, looking out at the crowd of his former supporters.

He was speaking to the remnants of his fanatical followers. "You see those buildings over there? Those are where I got elected. I told you all that I would build that wall, and I did it. But you never believed me. You were all about Hillary. You were always the #NeverTrumpers. You were too busy playing on your smartphones, and pretending that you were better than the rest of us. Well, I got you now, you worthless bums. I got you good."

Trump walked over to a young man sitting on the steps, who looked to be in his early 20s.

Trump grabbed the young man's face with both of his large hands. "You, son. You are the future. You are the one that is going to save this country. You are going to lead the way for the rest of us. You are going to lead the way for the Silent Majority. You are the future. You are the future, son. You are the future."

The young man nodded his head.

"You are the future, son. You are the future. You are the future."

Trump put the young man's face into his own, and he began to kiss him on the lips.

"You are the future, son. You are the future. You are the future."

Trump then backed off, and he looked at the rest of the crowd. "But you? You, I am going to cut your heads off and use them as target practice. You are a bunch of worthless idiots. You are all going to die. You are going to die. You are going to die. You are all going to die. You are all going to die."

The FBI Is Watching Trump Eat [The Black Storm]

The only thing worse would be if he was found guilty of treason and sentenced to death. And yet, he still had followers.

More than followers. They were his cult. And they were still with him.

It had been a long 6 years.

The whole world had been watching his every move, and the FBI had been watching him the whole time.

They knew every little detail about him.

They knew where he slept, and what he ate for breakfast.

They knew what movies he watched, and what music he listened to.

They knew where he lived, and they knew all of the goings on in his life.

They even knew his favorite color. Black.

All of this information was collected in the form of daily logs. Hundreds of pages of logs. Many of them were put together by the Director himself, as he was the one who was most likely to be able to piece together what was going on in the man's life, and how he was getting away with it.

It was a never ending mission. The Director was constantly on the move. He never stopped.

He was always on the run, always looking for something to make the next day worth living.

The Director had been a secret agent since the age of 21.

He had been one of the best in his class. He had an IQ of 186.

When he was 25, he was sent to Antarctica to deal with the strange creatures that had been unearthed there. He had been alone for a week.

He was almost to the end of his shift when he had heard a commotion. He thought it was the wind, so he ignored it.

The commotion continued. Then it got louder. Then it got closer.

He was about to head back to the airship when he heard someone call his name.

He turned and saw an old woman. She was wearing a black dress, and her hair was all white.

He had never seen anyone so old. She was over a hundred years old.

He had never seen anyone so old.

"You're a very old lady. Are you lost?" He asked her.

"Oh, no. I'm just on my way home. I live just up that way," she said, pointing to the north.

"I think I just heard a commotion"

“I'm sure I'll be home soon."

The Director followed her, as she walked in the opposite direction.

He followed her for a while, and then he realized that she was walking directly into a storm.

He looked around, and he could see that it was getting stronger.

He looked at her again. He didn't want to look scared, but he knew that he should.

She was the last person he wanted to meet in a storm.

"Hey, lady. Wait up!" He yelled. She kept walking, and the Director followed.

She was heading straight into a storm. The Director could see that.

He could see it coming. It was about to be bad.

It was about to be worse than any storm he had ever seen.

He ran to catch up to her, and she was still walking.

She didn't look back, and the Director was worried.

He had never seen anyone run into a storm like that. She was moving so fast.

"Ma'am, please wait!" The Director shouted, as he tried to catch up to her. She kept going.

The Director knew that he had to get to her before it was too late.

He ran as fast as he could. The storm was getting closer.

The Director was still about 50 yards behind her. He had never run that fast in his life.

He could feel his heart beating.

He could feel his body shaking.

He could feel his legs shaking.

He could feel his arms shaking.

He could see her in the distance, and she was running toward the center of the storm.

"Wait!" The Director yelled. He tried to stop her, but she just kept going.

He didn't know what to do. He tried to follow her, but she was running so fast.

He tried to stop her, but he was too slow.

He tried to hold on to her, but he couldn't.

She kept going, and the Director finally gave up.

He turned around and ran back to the airship. He knew that it was a losing battle.

He knew that she was going to get caught.

He knew that he couldn't stop her.

He knew that he couldn't follow her.

He ran back to the airship. He had never felt this way. He was so scared.

He was so scared for her. He was so scared that she was going to get caught.

He was so scared that she was going to die.

He was so scared that she was going to die. He was so scared that he couldn't breathe. He couldn't stop breathing.
He couldn't stop thinking. He was so scared that he didn't know what to do.

He was so scared that he didn't know what to say.

He was so scared that he didn't know what to say.

He was so scared that he didn't know what to do.

He was so scared that he didn't know what to say.

"I'm sorry," He said, "I'm so sorry. I don't know what I was thinking. I'm so sorry."

The Director had always been in control. He had always been in control.

He was in control of everything.

He had always been in control of everything.

He was in control of everything.

He was in control of everything.

He was in control of everything.

The Director's life was one of danger.

He was one of the best. He had the power.

He had the ability. He had the respect. He had the obedience.

He had the loyalty.

He had the support. He had the ability.

He had the power.

He had the respect.

He had the obedience.

He had the support. The Director was the best.

The Average American is Angry

The largest rioting city in the nation had been aflame for 2 days, and the country was still in shock.

While the fallout from the Trump presidency had been mostly positive, Trump had also left the FBI with a considerable amount of cash and a lot of resources, so it was easy to say that the outcome had been good for the country.

The problems that still remained were the problems that would need to be addressed by the new President.

The only way to fully explain the Trump presidency is to take the average American into the fold.

Trump is just an average American.

The average American is a working class man who has a job, but not a great one, and lives paycheck to paycheck, only able to afford the barest necessities for his family.

He feels oppressed by the establishment, and he feels that the political and financial powers in the nation are out to get him, and that he is unable to win against them because they have the power.

The average American hates the rich, but does not hate the poor because he is poor, and it is hard to hate somebody who has nothing.

The average American is a man who has been oppressed by the establishment and is unable to afford the barest necessities of life, and he is angry that he is so powerless.

He hates the rich, but he is also angry at the poor, because he sees them as being lazy, and being at the mercy of the rich.

The average American is a man who feels oppressed by the establishment and has lost hope in his own ability to affect change.

He feels helpless and hopeless, and he is angry and he feels entitled to be angry, because he is angry.

God Gets It [The Widows]

Trump's body had turned to water as the details of his crimes came to light.

The President had called in an Army Helicopter to pick him up from Camp David to allow him to be airlifted to the hospital, where the President would be treated for his severe kidney stone condition.

But, a massive storm struck the area and the helicopter had to abort the mission.

Trump was on his way to the hospital, when he was hit by lightning.

The President was in his golf cart, when a bolt of lightning struck him and he was instantly electrocuted.

The President was taken to the hospital, where he was pronounced dead.

He was 68.

The First Lady, Melania, had to be airlifted to the hospital, where she was treated for her shock.

It was too late for Trump's body to be revived, and she could not face the media to say what Trump's final words were.

Trump's last words were believed to be: "It was my honor to serve you, my beloved people."

The first thing the First Lady did upon arriving at the hospital was to be taken to Trump's bedroom.

She told the nurses she wanted to see the President's favorite painting of her, which was of the Adriatic.

The painting was on the wall of the bedroom.

The First Lady was in shock, but she composed herself.

The nurses asked her if she wanted a sedative, and she declined.

Melania Trump was greeted by the President's ex-wife, Ivana.

"What happened? What happened?" Ivana asked.

"I don't know. It just happened," Melania replied.

"What did he say to you?" Ivana asked.

"He didn't say anything," Melania replied.

"What did he say to you?" Ivana asked.

"I don't know," Melania replied.

Ivana was devastated.

"I don't know what to do," Ivana said. "He's the love of my life. What will I do?"

"It's okay," Melania replied. "I will take care of him."

Ivana began to cry.

"I will take care of him," Melania said. "You go see him."

Ivana and Melania cried and hugged.

"I love you," Ivana said.

"I love you too," Melania said.

Ivana and Melania left the hospital.

The next thing Melania did was go to the Oval Office and pick up Trump's Bible, which was on the desk.

She read a passage from it to the nurses. "You will be with the Lord forever. And I will see you again," Melania read.

The nurses all smiled.

Melania put the Bible back on the desk.

Next, Melania went to the closet, where she found some clothes.

"I don't know what to do," Ivana said. "I can't just leave him alone."

"Don't worry. I'll take care of him," Melania said.

Melania put on some clothes, grabbed the President's hat, and left the room.

Ivana was not sure what to do, but she knew that Melania was the type of person that would take care of her husband.

"I'll do what she says," Ivana thought.

Melania was on the third floor of the hospital.

She went into Trump's bathroom and washed his face.

Trump had a large collection of Trump products in the bathroom.

Melania picked up a Trump Tie and some Trump shaving cream and put them on the counter.

"I love you," Melania said to Trump.

Trump did not reply.

The doorbell rang.

Melania went to the front door and opened it.

"Mrs. Trump?" a man asked.

"Yes?" Melania replied.

"I'm sorry to bother you," the man said.

"It's okay. Come on in," Melania said.

The man entered the house and took a seat. "I'm sorry to bother you," the man said.

"It's okay. It's okay," Melania said.

"I'm sorry to bother you," the man said. "It's important."

"What's important?" Melania asked.

"I'm a Federal Agent," the man replied. "I'm with the F.B.I. I'm looking for information on your husband. I believe he has been dead for a while."

"Oh," Melania replied. "Well, he is."

"You're kidding," the man said.

"No," Melania replied. "I'm not. He is. He's been dead for a while."

"I'm sorry to bother you," the man said. "I just need to talk to him."

"I'm sorry. He's not here," Melania replied.

"Where is he?" the man asked.

"He's in the hospital," Melania replied.

"The hospital?" the man asked.

"Yes," Melania replied. "He's been dead for a while."

"I'm sorry to bother you," the man said. "I just need to talk to him."

One More Speech

Trump's impeachment, followed by the loss of his political career, was the beginning of the end of the Trump brand.

It was not about whether he could be impeached or not.

It was about how the entire world would view the United States of America.

Trump's brand was on the brink of destruction, and the world was staring at it's end.

"This is a great day for the American people," Trump said from the Rose Garden as the crowd began to chant "Impeach 45!"

"It's a great day for the American people. The impeachment was a horrible thing for our country. I'm not happy. I've been saying for two years, I don't care who it is, 'He's not gonna be able to beat Hillary Clinton.' That was proven right. It was a horrible thing for our country, but I'm not surprised. This is a horrible day for our country. It's a great day for the American people. They've been waiting a long time for this day, for this victory. I can't wait to get back to work. I'll see you guys in a little while. Thank you very much."

The crowd began to boo and chant "We love you!" and "USA! USA!"

"So, we've just completed the first impeachment in our history. The case is closed. It's over. It's over. I just want to thank God for our country. We're about to start the greatest economy in the history of the world. We have the most stable, secure, and greatest military in the world. We have the best economy in the world. We have the best jobs in the world. We have the best unemployment in the world. I love America. I love our country. We love our military. We love our vets. We love our country. We love our flag."

The Insanity Of It All [Trump Retires To Enjoy A Cohiba]

Trump was a narcissistic egomaniac.

He was the very definition of an alpha male.

He was also a pathological liar.

He did not tell the truth, and when he did, it was so full of logical contradictions that he could never maintain a coherent narrative.

This was the first time a President had ever been impeached.

The Founding Fathers had not even considered this in their wildest dreams.

And now, it was happening, and the world was in an uproar.

The President had not only lied about what had happened with the Russian Collusion, but he had lied about the fact that he had been in charge of it all.

He had lied about the fact that the FBI had been investigating him for obstruction of justice.

He had lied about the fact that he had been so insanely reckless with our national security that he had directly endangered the lives of the American people.

He had lied about the fact that he had caused the death of an American in the assassination attempt on his life.

He had lied about the fact that he had lied to the people.

The man that had to be the most insane of all, however, was the man that the media was trying to pin all of this on.

The man that had built his entire political career on lies was the man that they were trying to pin everything on.

And it didn't matter how many times Trump's team tried to show him the evidence, it didn't matter how many times his family tried to get him to see what was happening, the man himself would never believe it.

And now, he was losing it.

The room was still spinning as Trump stood up and started walking toward the door. His former Attorney General, William Barr, and his former Chief of Staff, John Kelly, stood up to follow him. The press was scrambling to get the questions they had prepared, and Trump started walking toward the door.

"Mr. President," they said. "We are going to need a moment of your time. We have a few questions for you."

"Why would you want to talk to me?" Trump asked, as he reached for the door.

"Mr. President, we have not come here to discuss your administration, or your decisions as President. We have come here to discuss your impeachment."

Trump looked at them and smiled. "Oh, I see."

"Mr. President, do you think that you would be removed from office if you were not President?"

"I don't know," Trump said, as he leaned against the door. "I guess I don't see why I should be removed from office."

"Mr. President, do you think that the Senate would remove you from office if you were not President?"

"I don't know," Trump said. "I guess I don't see why they would."

"Mr. President, do you think that the House of Representatives would impeach you if you were not President?"

"I don't know," Trump said. "I guess I don't see why they would."

"Mr. President, do you think that you would be removed from office if you were not President?"

"I don't know," Trump said, as he turned the doorknob. "I guess I don't see why I would."

"Mr. President, would you be willing to testify in an impeachment hearing?"

"I don't know," Trump said, as he opened the door. "I guess I don't see why I would."

The press was furious.

They had been trying to pin him down for months. They had been trying to pin him down for years.

But the man they were trying to pin him down to, the man they were trying to pin him down on the lies of, the man they were trying to pin him down on the truth of, he was never going to say anything.

The room was now empty, except for Trump's former Chief of Staff, who was sitting down. Trump looked at him and said, "John, I just want to say that I am so sorry. I'm so sorry that I have to do this to you. I am so sorry. But I have to go. I have to go."

Trump's former Attorney General, William Barr, was sitting down as well.

"Mr. President, do you think that you would be removed from office if you were not President?"

"I don't know," Trump said. "I guess I don't see why I would."

The two of them looked at each other, and Trump just nodded.

The next day, the President was sitting on the back patio of his new home in Bedminster, New Jersey, and enjoying a cigar.

He had just returned from a trip to the Middle East, and was anxious to relax.

"John, I am going to have to have you come out and get me a few cigars," Trump said.

"Mr. President, I'm happy to," Kelly said. "I've been out there for a while. But I'm not sure I can get you a Cohiba."

"That's fine," Trump said. "I don't care. I just want a cigar."

"Okay, sir," Kelly said. "I'll see what I can do."

"I'm sorry about that," Trump said. "I really am. I am so sorry that I have to do this to you."

Kelly didn't say anything. He didn't need to. He just nodded.

"I just want to tell you, John," Trump said. "I don't know if I can ever do it again."

Kelly nodded.

"I don't know if I can do it again," Trump said. "I don't know if I can do it anymore."

Trump Writes His Prophecies and Gloats Like An Egomaniac

And it was only going to get worse.*

That morning, the President awoke at his suburban Virginia home. A small flock of small birds had been flying over the lawn, chirping merrily, the gentle morning breeze drifting over the lawn. The birds were chirping incessantly, but Trump had been awake for hours. He had been thinking about the night before, and how he had not slept a wink.

"I have to do it. There's no other choice," he told himself as he climbed out of bed.

He grabbed a small black briefcase, a staple in his closet. Opening it, he removed a few items. There were several pages of notes scribbled down in his own hand. His thoughts. His concerns. His hopes. It was a book. A book he had been working on for years, a book that would blow the doors off the world. A book that would unite the masses of the country and make him a living legend. A book that would change the world. The book was called "The Trump Prophecies."

"The Trump Prophecies" was a book that was not only written by Donald J. Trump, but also by his mother, his wife, his children, his lawyers, his friends, his family, his business associates, and his numerous other friends and family. The book was compiled by Trump's son, Eric Trump, and his daughter Ivanka Trump. The book had been a massive success, and was one of the best selling books of the year.

As he looked at the pages of his book, he was absolutely awestruck. This was truly a masterpiece, and it had taken him the better part of a year to write. He had never written anything like this before. It was a complete masterpiece. He had to stop thinking about it, or he would never be able to continue writing.

He took the pages into the living room, and began to write. He was in the zone. He was on a roll. His words flowed from his fingertips as he scribbled notes and continued to write. He had a blank book. He could not believe that he was actually doing it. It had taken him this long to get here. He was making history. He had been writing for hours, and now he had to sleep for a while.

He walked over to his study, and placed the book on the desk. There were at least a dozen other books in his study. He had an entire library of books. He walked over to his study and closed the door. He placed his briefcase on his desk, and turned on his computer. He logged into his personal blog, and saw that there were over 200,000 hits.

"My God," he said to himself.

He had never imagined this. His blog was one of the most popular on the web. The hits were endless. He had to think about that.

"I'm the most popular President in history," he thought to himself. "I'm the most popular man in the history of the world. I'm the most popular President in the history of the world. I'm the most popular man in the history of the world."

He was absolutely in awe of his own genius.

He had always known that he was a smart man. He had always known that he was a talented man. He had always known that he was a good man. But he had never imagined that he could be a great man. A great President. A great man of history.

He was the President of the United States. He was the most powerful man in the world. He was the most wealthy man in the world. He was the most powerful man in the history of the world. And he was the most popular man in the history of the world. He had always been the smartest man in the room. But he had never imagined that he could be the smartest man in the room.

"I'm the smartest man in the room," he thought to himself.

He sat down at his desk and began to write. His thoughts were flowing like a river. He could not believe what he was doing.

"I am the President of the United States," he thought. "I am the most powerful man in the world. I am the most wealthy man in the world. I am the smartest man in the room. I am the most popular man in the world."

He was sitting in his home office. He was on his computer, and he was writing. He had never imagined that he could write like this. He had never imagined that he could write like this.

"I am the most powerful man in the world," he thought. "I am the most wealthy man in the world. I am the smartest man in the room. I am the most popular man in the world."

He was the President of the United States.

**[Ed note: The Gpt-J-6B appears to have made a valid prophecy here. -MCW,D (or I did.)]*

---

*The John Bolton Gambit [Just Who is President Here?]**

Trump's resurrection was both unprecedented and miraculous.

In less than a year, he had gone from a fringe candidate to the leader of the free world. He had created a government of his own design. He had appointed a cabinet of his own design. He had made a Supreme Court of his own design. He had enacted his own immigration laws. He had created a new, more lenient law enforcement approach. He had started a new trade policy, and his tariffs were proving to be a powerful weapon against our enemies. He had created a new space program. He had initiated a new nuclear policy that would secure America's future. He had changed our culture.

He had done all of this and he had done it all with a bunch of buffoons as his cabinet.

But I was not one of them. I was a lifelong Republican, but I was not fooled by Trump. He was a pathological liar, and he lied to me every day.

I could see it. I could smell it. I could taste it.

He was a master manipulator, and I could see through his game.

I was even starting to like him a little. He was a con man, but he was also a master manipulator, and he was playing a very clever game.

I was on the outside looking in, but I was still looking in. I was still looking for the key to the Trump puzzle. I was just about to crack the code when I received the call.

"Hello, Mr. Bolton."

"Hello, Donald."

"How are you, sir?"

"I'm fine, Donald. How are you?"

"Oh, I'm doing great. I'm doing great."

"Good. Good to hear that."

"So, how is the Presidency?"

"Oh, it's great, Donald. It's great. I can't say enough about how great it is."

"Good to hear it. Listen, I've been thinking about you a lot recently. I really want you to consider running for President again in 2020, I think you would be great."

"I appreciate that, Donald. I really appreciate that."

"So, what do you say, Mr. Bolton?"

"I say you're a moron, Donald. I mean, I've known you for a long time, and I've never known you to be a moron. And I'm not going to say that anymore."

**[Ed note: I did edit this one for context, as the AI gets conversations muddled sometimes.] The AI really did have Bolton as President calling the deposed Trump a moron, just needed that to be clear.]*

The Good, The Bad, & The Ugly [Forcefeed Bigotry on the AI]

And now Trump is gone.

The clown prince of DC will be missed.

The Good:

What a damn show. From the ridiculous 'Alone with the Clown' headline to the ridiculous tweets, Trump's last 6 years of running the show were one hell of a show. Every day there was a new spectacle, and each one was better than the last. Trump was never boring, and when the 'not so good' news came out, it was like a punch in the stomach, and you knew he was not going to recover from it. For those who missed the show, here is a recap of his last 6 years in office.

The Bad:

Trump has done nothing for America.

He never had a plan. He never cared about the people. He cared about himself. He cared about his family. He cared about his supporters. But he didn't care about the country. He didn't care about the poor. He didn't care about the middle class. He didn't care about the common man. He didn't care about the constitution. He didn't care about the rule of law. He didn't care about the war on terror. He didn't care about the peace process. He didn't care about anyone but himself.

There is a reason Trump never has a plan. He doesn't care about the plan. He doesn't care about anything other than his own interests. He doesn't care about the people, or the country. He doesn't care about the constitution. He doesn't care about the war on terror. He doesn't care about the peace process. He doesn't care about the rule of law. He doesn't care about anything other than his own interests.

Trump has done nothing for America.

His is a perfect example of the narcissist. He cares about himself. He cares about his family. He cares about his supporters. He cares about his name. He cares about money. He cares about himself. He cares about his own interests. He doesn't care about the people. He doesn't care about the country. He doesn't care about the constitution. He doesn't care about the war on terror. He doesn't care about the peace process. He doesn't care about anyone but himself.

The Ugly:*

He was a racist.

Trump was the epitome of everything that is wrong with America. He was a racist. He didn't care about the black people. He didn't care about the Jewish people. He didn't care about the Hispanic people. He didn't care about the Muslim people. He didn't care about the Asian people. He didn't care about the white people. He didn't care about the LGBT people. He didn't care about women. He didn't care about the disabled. He didn't care about anyone but himself.

He was a racist.

He was a bigot.

**[Ed note: I added "The Ugly:" as a prompt because I had a hunch the AI would interpret that as a call to add a bit about the racism Trump evinced.*

Temperature Turned Up to 0.83 [He Boils Alive in AI Juice]

The Democrats and their allies in the media had made no secret of their intention to take out Trump with any means necessary, and they were out to prove to the nation that they were more than willing to do just that. It was only a matter of time before the entire apparatus of the government, including the Supreme Court, came down on the side of the anti-Trump media and their allies in the political establishment.

Trump had been in office for about 6 months and he had already done enough damage to the Democratic Party, to the rule of law, and to America's reputation in the world. It was too late for the country to recover from all of the harm he had already done. In one final act of narcissistic grandiosity, Trump made the mistake of giving a press conference to announce that he had finally discovered the perfect plan to end his Presidency and bring the country together, right before the greatest threat to his presidency ever occurred.

In that moment of weakness, Trump revealed to the entire world just how truly mentally unstable he was. The current media had already been working on this for months, preparing for the day when Trump would make the decision to remove himself from the presidency, but they were surprised by just how badly he screwed up. Instead of just going away quietly, Trump put the whole thing out there. He made it so clear just how much he was suffering that his own mind had completely broken. He revealed how unstable he was, how easily he could snap and how that snap could be fatal to the country. The media, and the Democratic Party, realized that they had to stop Trump from making any more mistakes, because the consequences of the next one could be life-changing.

Meanwhile, back in reality, former President Hillary Clinton had just been found guilty of lying to Congress, for which she had already been fined, and her lawyers had just filed a motion to have the case thrown out. The defense team had already pointed out that the information was already in the public domain, and that the fact that she had intentionally withheld the information was already well-known. They were making a strong case for her to have been found innocent, but the prosecution had a mountain of evidence to prove that she was guilty, and that evidence was never going to be thrown out. The defense team was going to have to spend millions of dollars, and a year of their lives, to get her acquitted.

The media and the Democratic Party were becoming increasingly worried. They had a lot riding on the outcome of this trial, but the defense was doing a good job of exposing just how corrupt the prosecution had been. They were having a hard time selling their narrative that Clinton was the victim of a 'right wing conspiracy' when the prosecution had just been caught red-handed conspiring with the right wing media. All of the evidence was out in the open. Clinton was going to be found guilty, and the public was becoming increasingly aware of just how corrupt the system had been. The Republicans were in disarray, and the Democrats were about to win back the House of Representatives, and the Senate. The Republicans were counting on the courts to save them from what was shaping up to be a political catastrophe.

As the Trump Presidency fell apart, the Republicans were losing the messaging war. Trump was doing more damage to the GOP than Clinton had done in her entire Presidency, and the Democrats were winning the messaging war. The Republicans were about to lose control of the Senate, and the House, and the Supreme Court was about to be turned into a super-partisan body that had become completely unaccountable. The media was pushing impeachment harder and harder, and the Republicans were about to lose their last chance at winning the Presidency in 2020. The Supreme Court, which had become a partisan body, was also about to become completely unaccountable.

In the midst of all of this chaos, Trump made the mistake of giving a press conference. He wanted to explain his plan for ending the Presidency, and he wanted to convince the nation that he was mentally stable enough to be president. He also wanted to reassure the public that he was the kind of President that would never do anything to intentionally harm the country. He was being overly optimistic. Trump was a narcissistic psychopath. He believed that his personality was so perfectly suited for the job of being President that he was going to be able to do whatever he wanted, and nobody was going to stop him. Trump had completely lost his mind, and he wanted everyone to know just how unstable he was.

Trump thought he could just give a press conference, and that would be the end of it. He couldn't have been more wrong. The press conference was the tipping point. The press conference was when the final straw broke the camel's back. The press conference was when Trump finally lost the ability to control himself. Trump was so narcissistic that he believed that he could say whatever he wanted, and it wouldn't matter, because the press conference would be seen as just another one of his gaffes. He was so narcissistic that he believed that he could get away with everything, because nobody was going to hold him accountable. Trump had so much anger in him that he was unable to control it. Trump couldn't control his rage, and it was getting out of control. Trump wanted to show the world that he was mentally stable, but he couldn't stop himself from saying things that were unacceptable.

Trump wanted to control the narrative, but his anger was getting the better of him. Trump's inability to control himself was the final straw. Trump's anger and his inability to control himself caused him to snap. After the press conference, Trump's actions became increasingly erratic, and he began doing more and more things that were completely unacceptable. Trump was on the verge of losing the Republican Party. Trump had caused enough damage to the GOP that the GOP was going to lose the House of Representatives in 2018. Trump had caused enough damage to the GOP that the GOP was going to lose the Senate in 2018. Trump was about to lose the Presidency in 2020. Trump was going to do everything he could to destroy the GOP, and the Republicans were about to lose the House of Representatives, the Senate, the Supreme Court, and the Presidency.

The Democrats were watching Trump's antics with interest. They were about to retake the House, and they were about to retake the Senate. They were about to win the Presidency in 2020, and they were about to win back the Supreme Court. The Democrats knew that Trump was a threat to the GOP, and they knew that he was a threat to the country. The Democrats were watching Trump's antics with interest. They knew that Trump was a threat to the country. Trump's antics were increasing in intensity, and he was about to lose control of himself.

Trump wasn't going to be able to stop himself from doing anything, and his anger was getting out of control.

About The Author

Matthew Chenoweth Wright iw a poet and musician, as well as experimental writer and Artificial Intelligence researcher. His band, eNuminous & Archimedes has a handful of musics, all available at www.enuminousandarchimedes.com

This is his third work of AI writings. His other work include:

The Dancing Penguins
The Candle That Burns Down to the Core of the World

On The Water
Fron Under eyelids
The Floating Laughter of the Harlequin's Anti-Gravity Brain
Alphabetical Verse

www.ingramcontent.com/pod-product-compliance
Lightning Source LLC
LaVergne TN
LVHW060838170826
845678LV00007B/1812

9798847251044